THE TOY SHOP
OF TERROR

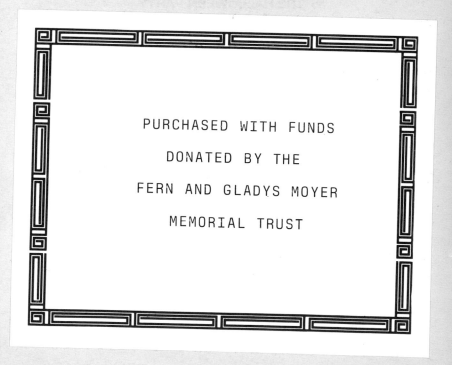

Don't miss these

CHOOSE YOUR OWN
NIGHTMARE

titles from Bantam Books:

CHOOSE YOUR OWN NIGHTMARE #18

THE TOY SHOP OF TERROR

by Laban Carrick Hill

Illustrated by Bill Schmidt

An R. A. Montgomery Book

BANTAM BOOKS

NEW YORK · TORONTO · LONDON · SYDNEY · AUCKLAND

RL 4, age 008–012

THE TOY SHOP OF TERROR
A Bantam Book/December 1997

CHOOSE YOUR OWN NIGHTMARE® is a registered trademark of
Bantam Doubleday Dell Books for Young Readers,
a division of Bantam Doubleday Dell Publishing Group, Inc.
Registered in U.S. Patent and Trademark Office and elsewhere.

Cover and interior illustrations by Bill Schmidt.
Cover and interior design by Beverly Leung.

ISBN 0-553-48458-3

Published simultaneously in the United States and Canada.

Bantam Books are published by Bantam Books, a division of
Bantam Doubleday Dell Publishing Group, Inc. Its trademark,
consisting of the words "Bantam Books" and the portrayal of a
rooster, is Registered in U.S. Patent and Trademark Office and in
other countries. Marca Registrada. Bantam Books, 1540 Broadway,
New York, New York 10036.

PRINTED IN THE UNITED STATES OF AMERICA

OPM   0   9   8   7   6   5   4   3   2   1

THE TOY SHOP
OF TERROR

WARNING!

You have probably read books where scary things happen to people. Well, in *Choose Your Own Nightmare*, you're right in the middle of the action. The scary things are happening to you!

'Tis the season . . . for getting SCARED! The new toy store in town's got great stuff . . . but you aren't too sure about the people who work there. There's something weird going on. . . .

Don't forget—YOU control your fate. Only you can decide what happens. Follow the instructions at the bottom of each page. The thrills and chills that happen to you will depend on your choices!

Have you been good this year? Well, we have a little present for you. Turn to page 1 . . . and *CHOOSE YOUR OWN NIGHTMARE!*

A crisp breeze whips around the school yard, sending wayward leaves into little whirlpools. You pull up your jacket zipper and glance at the gray sky.

"Think it's going to snow?" you ask your best friend, Evan Tomchin. "I'm freezing."

Evan sinks his hands deeper into his pockets. He's wearing only a jean jacket with a patch that says "Munch On" stitched to the right shoulder. He has it buttoned up to his neck. "If I thought it was, I would have worn my down parka." He stomps his feet on the sidewalk.

The two of you hurry down Elm Street against a frigid wind. Elm Street used to be lined with giant elms, but twenty years ago the trees all died of Dutch elm disease. The bare street provides no protection from the icy air.

Evan points down Pell Street. "Let's take Pell to Maple and then cut back to our houses," he suggests. "There won't be as much wind."

"I'm right behind you," you answer.

Evan pushes you in front of him. "No, *I'm* right behind *you*," he says. "You make the perfect shield against the wind."

Turn to the next page.

2

You spin and get behind him. "You're the one with the fat head," you reply. "You could block out the sun with that forehead."

"Very funny," Evan sneers. His head isn't really that big, considering his size. He's a good six inches taller than everyone else in your class. You like having the biggest kid as your best friend. It makes you feel safe.

"Come on. I'm turning into an icicle," you say. The two of you tromp four blocks down Pell and turn right up Maple. Maple Street runs through the business district of Freeville. But at this time of day, the street is usually deserted.

That's why you're so surprised when you look down the street and see a huge crowd forming at the corner of Mission and Maple.

You nudge Evan. "Hey, what's going on up there?"

"Looks like the line for Santa Claus at the mall," he replies. It's the week before Thanksgiving.

You and Evan walk toward the crowd. When you see what everyone is gathering around, you stop dead in your tracks.

Go to page 3.

Just ahead, the upper branches of Freeville's famous Camperdown Maple are lit up like a Christmas tree. But it's what's below the lights that really shocks you. A low building that looks like a castle has been constructed around the bottom half of the tree. People are laughing and milling all around it.

The Camperdown Maple is the oldest and largest tree in town, with a 215-inch trunk circumference. It's stood at the corner of Maple and Mission in front of the old church as long as anyone can remember. Everyone wondered what would happen to the Camperdown Maple when the church closed last year. Now you see what's happened to it.

And you're not pleased . . . or are you?

"Cool!" Evan says.

Turn to page 4.

4

You're not so sure. The top of the tree is covered with lights, and the trunk is almost completely enclosed by one of the most marvelous buildings you've ever seen. The building is decorated with spinning wheels and electric trains circling each floor.

"I think it's a castle," you whisper in awe.

"And look what it's made of," Evan responds.

The castle is made of rock candy, with a huge gingerbread drawbridge. Dozens of people are hurrying back and forth across the bridge, their arms full of the most spectacular toys you've ever seen.

"How did they build this so fast?" you ask. "I mean, nothing was here last week."

"Pretty cool, huh?" Evan replies. He doesn't seem to care how long it took to build the castle. He just wants to check out the toys.

"Let's go," he calls, dashing to the drawbridge.

Flip to page 29.

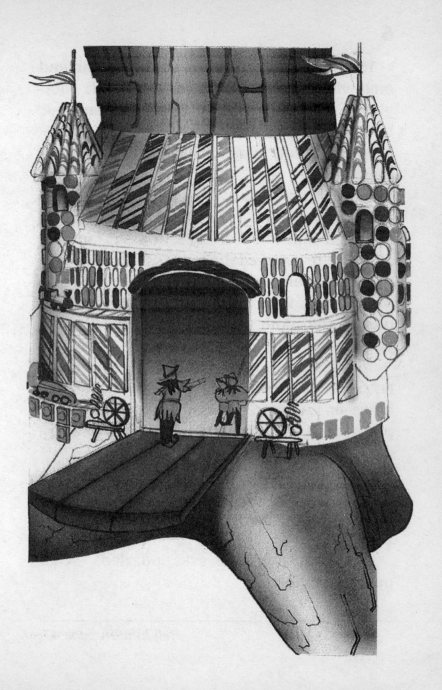

6

The next day after school you grab Evan and make him accompany you to town hall.

"But I like the toy store," Evan protests.

You give him a withering look.

He raises his hands. "Okay, you win," he says.

The town clerk is a prim, meticulous, balding man. He wears a plaid shirt and jeans. You expected him to be dressed in a suit and tie, and you're relieved he's not. Suits and ties make you nervous.

He smiles from behind a long counter that divides the room in half. "What can I do for you?"

Your side of the counter is completely empty. No chairs. No tables. Nothing. His side, however, is cluttered like an old attic. Stacks of papers and file cabinets are packed in every available space.

Nervously you approach the counter.

You read his name tag: John Free. "Yes. I'd like to get a copy of the building permit for the new toy store."

"New toy store?" he asks, puzzled. "What new toy store?"

Tell him on page 43.

"Never mind," you say sheepishly, as you stare up at the ugly elf. You turn and head back toward the ball pit, but on the way you decide to bag it. Evan can find his own way home. You're tired of all this kid stuff.

Four weeks later, it's Christmas morning. Excited, you hurry to the living room. "Mom! Dad!" you call. "Hurry up!"

Once your mom and dad sit down with their coffee, you tear into your presents.

The first one is from Grandma: flannel pajamas with feet. She still thinks you're three years old. Next is a large package from your mom and dad. You're very excited—you can tell this is your big present. As you tear it open, you scream in delight. It's the mountain-bike kit you've been asking for.

"I can't believe you got me this!" you shout, as you run to the garage to get your tool kit.

Your parents just laugh as they watch you put the bike together.

It takes longer than you expected, but in three hours the bike is finally ready for a road test. You push it toward the front door. You want to ride over to Evan's house first.

Go to Evan's on page 79.

8

"You don't have an uncle Melvin," you tell him.

Evan shrugs. "Yeah, I do. You just never met him. Hey," he says, switching gears. "You want to head over to my house and play some video games?"

"Nah, I think I'm going to go home," you answer, really disappointed that he's lying to you.

"But I just got Wally Wimp," he says pleadingly.

This stops you. Wally Wimp is a cool new video game. A strong little troll, Wally Wimp, must climb a huge mountain to get to a cache of gold. Along the way, snowstorms, avalanches, rock slides, herds of mountain goats, and evil elves try to stop him.

"When did you get that?" you ask suspiciously. He didn't have Wally Wimp yesterday.

Evan ignores your question. "I've made it to level thirteen already," he brags.

Turn to page 33.

You pick a door and knock. No answer.

You try another door. Again, no answer.

You try a third door. Still no answer. This time, however, you try the handle. It's unlocked. "Hello?" you call as you slowly open the door.

The room is dark, but somehow you don't feel alone. You hear a whirring sound. Or is it breathing? You can't tell.

Nervously you feel along the wall for a light switch. You find one and flip it on.

A bright spotlight washes the room with light. You are temporarily blinded. You rub your eyes. When you open them, you can't believe what you see.

Hundreds of little tin windup cars scurry about the floor. At first they seem to be trying to find a place to hide in the empty room. But then they all turn toward you.

Better turn to page 44.

The cake is delicious. By the time you swallow your second helping, however, you begin to feel funny. Light-headed. As if you could float across the room. The colors of the other kids' clothes seem brighter, and the music in the room sounds cheerier.

Something was in that cake. Too much sugar? Your mom is always warning you about eating too much sugar. She says you get hyper. But you don't care. You feel great! You join in a game of hopscotch.

The day whips by. You're so caught up in your game of hopscotch that you don't notice anything. This is really strange, because you've never been a hopscotch fan before. You've always thought the game was for babies. You prefer sports like soccer. But now all you want to do is throw your stone and hop up and down the grid. You're not even aware of any other kids playing with you. The memory of your best friend, Evan, has been completely wiped away. So has the memory of . . .

Check out page 42.

"Just kidding." Evan laughs as he pulls off the goggles. He hands the goggles to you. "Want to try?"

"I'm not sure," you say haltingly.

"I've *got* to have this," Evan says, taking the suit off. "It's the coolest game I've ever played. And it's only fifty bucks. All I have to do is figure out how to get fifty bucks."

You glance across the room at the video section. "I think I'll stick to regular video games." You go over to them.

"Hey!" Evan calls. "Are you sure?"

You nod. To your amazement, you spot the Wally Wimp game. Cool! "Evan! They've got Wally Wimp. I can't believe they've got it!"

"Great!" Evan joins you. "But you gotta try the virtual-reality suit." He pushes you back across the room and then returns to the video games. You pick up the suit.

Then you spot one of the toy shop's workers standing by the door. Hoping that Evan doesn't see you, you hurry over to the worker. "Excuse me."

A little woman with rosy cheeks and pointy ears looks up at you. "Yes?"

Turn to page 24.

The elves quickly tie you up and lock you in a closet. You sit cramped in the dark for what seems like hours. Over the next few days you think you're going to go insane from hunger and thirst, but somehow you survive.

The police find you the day after Christmas. You try to explain that you were kidnapped by elves, but they don't believe you. They're more concerned with trying to solve the disappearance of Evan and his entire family.

Unfortunately no one solves that mystery, and no one will believe what you have to say about it. No matter how persistent you are.

The End

14

Next, the tinny strains of "Pop Goes the Weasel" catch your attention. You see a giant, colorful, grinning jack-in-the-box popping up and surprising people. It springs wildly back and forth. You duck as its arm sweeps above your head. You could have sworn the jack was throwing a left hook.

A crowd forms when the jack-in-the-box waves and says, "Howdya do?" Then the jack bounces back into its box.

You frown. Something is not right about this jack. For one thing, it's too big. And it has a wicked punch.

You wait to see it pop out again as the crowd turns away. To your surprise, the top of the box cracks open just a few inches. Then the jack's hand slowly slips out.

The hand reaches into a woman's purse. She doesn't notice. Instead, she's distracted by a giant rubber acrobat stretching across the length of the castle.

Better check out page 69.

You duck your head, and the spell of the colors breaks. You begin sliding down a chute and land in a big pit of balls right beside the place where you opened the door.

Evan has joined a crowd watching a huge black stuffed spider shoot a thread up toward the ceiling.

You wave to get Evan's attention, and he comes over. "You've got to try this ride!" you say, leading him to the mirrored door on the right.

"What ride?" Evan says.

"Go through the right door and up the escalator. I'll wait for you here," you tell him. Evan shrugs and follows your instructions.

You can't wait to see his face when he lands in the ball pit. You wait five minutes. Ten minutes. Still no Evan. Fifteen minutes. Half an hour!

You panic. You've got to do something. Maybe he came out in another place and went home. Maybe he's stuck.

If you decide to go to his house, turn to page 41.

If you look for help, turn to page 78.

If you take the ride again, turn to page 86.

Your mom agrees to wait until daylight to investigate the castle.

You and your mom go back to bed. As usual, the alarm clock goes off at 6:30 A.M. You automatically slam down the snooze button for an extra ten minutes.

BUUZZZZZZZ! That ten minutes passes fast. The clock must've speeded up. It seems as if it always does when you hit the snooze button. You groan and stretch, making such a racket that you sound like a herd of wild animals.

"Sounds like you're waking up from the Ice Age," your mom calls from the hallway as she passes by. "Get up!"

Slowly you crawl out of bed. You hate morning light. It makes you squint. You feel your way across the room and skirt a few obstacles like a chair and schoolbooks, but you plow right into the leg of your desk.

"Ouch!" you scream in agonizing pain. Your big toe throbs. "What a knucklehead," you chide yourself. You can't believe you've done something so stupid.

Open your eyes on page 31.

Finally the store quiets down. You and Evan wait for what seems like another half hour before you crack the door.

The main floor of the store is dark and quiet. "Come on," Evan whispers. You follow him out of the closet and across the floor to a large table. Dozens of laser guns are scattered across it. Next to it stands a small black box. Evan flips the switch on the box's side. It hums with energy.

"Watch this!" Evan picks up a laser gun. He reaches down and pushes a button on the box.

The box projects a 3-D holographic Old West gunslinger in the air.

"Draw!" it shouts.

Evan quickly points his laser gun and fires. The gunslinger is faster and blasts Evan. In shock you watch Evan fly across the shop. His head crashes through the glass doors of a large shelf.

"Too slow," the gunslinger drawls.

Go to page 37.

"Yeah, Mom," you answer. You glance out the window and see that it's still dark outside. But that's no surprise, since the days are so short this time of year. It's always dark in the morning, and it's nearly dark when you get out of school. "What time is it?"

"It's two A.M.," your mom answers as she bursts into your room. "Evan's mom just called. Evan never came home!"

"What?" you answer, shocked. You hop out of bed and pull on your robe. Then you follow your mom downstairs.

"The police are here," your mom says on the steps.

Huh? What did you do now? You can't think of anything you've done wrong . . . lately.

There was that window you broke last month, but you already paid for it to be fixed with two months' worth of your allowance.

Hurry to page 77.

You wake up hours later. Your head really hurts. The last thing you remember is falling— first, Wally falling off the mountain, then you falling. Were you climbing the mountain, or was Wally? You open your eyes to see where to begin climbing the mountain again.

"Don't move," commands a faraway voice.

You look around to see where you are. It's not a mountain. You're not a cartoon troll.

"Sit still," says a warm, friendly voice. It sounds like one of the elves from the toy castle. This doesn't make sense, but then Evan conking you on the head defies all logic. He's your best friend. Why would he hurt you?

You're in a dimly lit room that's crammed with all kinds of stuffed animals. And the person leaning over you is big and round and fluffy. It's a stuffed toy!

You blink. It's not a stuffed toy. It's a little man dressed in red.

Find out who he is on page 72.

20

You push the cart back through the door to the storage room. The place is bustling with activity. You approach a plump little woman with rosy red cheeks who is, of course, dressed in green.

"I can't seem to find the loading dock," you explain.

She shakes her head and smiles. "You go out to the sales floor, and I'll take this cart to the dock. It's hard to find."

"But what am I supposed to do?" you ask. "I haven't been trained yet."

A worried look crosses her face. "You don't want to be working here."

Turn to page 53.

You figure your mom will protect you from any harm, so you follow her to the toy store. To your surprise, the castle is still open. Flashing colored lights cover the edges of the building and the limbs of the Camperdown Maple. "Pop Goes the Weasel" blasts out of giant speakers.

"Isn't there a town ordinance against this?" your mom asks, irritated. "They shouldn't be open at this time of night. This must be illegal. I'm calling town hall first thing in the morning." She pulls into the public parking lot next door. The two of you march to the castle's entrance. Two elflike people are tossing glitter into the air.

"It looks like New Year's Eve," you crack, as the glitter falls on your mom but misses you.

Your mom doesn't respond. She's obviously angry at all the noise and commotion they're making at this time of the morning.

To your surprise, however, the place is packed. Dozens of people are milling about inside and playing with toys.

Check it out on page 38.

Reflexively, you roll to the right. And it's a good thing you do, because the spot where you were just lying is now a gaping hole.

Without thinking, you leap up and dive toward Evan. He's much larger than you, but you catch him at the knees and knock him off balance. As he's falling, you rip off his goggles and helmet and pin your elbow into his throat.

"Whaaaa . . . ," Evan gurgles.

He struggles for a second, then goes limp. He drops the laser gun and raises his hands over his head in submission.

"What's gotten into you?" you scream.

Evan takes two deep breaths. "I don't know. I just put on this space suit, and I went crazy."

"Evan!" his mom says sharply from the doorway. Her left arm is bleeding. "What *has* gotten into you?"

Evan turns toward her. "I don't know, Mom," he says apologetically. "It's like the suit took control of me when I put the helmet on."

"Obviously, it's not a toy," Mrs. Tomchin says. "I'll return it first thing tomorrow."

Is this a good idea?
If you think it is, go to page 88.

If you don't think so, turn to page 76.

Evan pulls you through a door into a dimly lit room. Laser lights shoot back and forth. All sorts of high-tech toys blink and make weird noises. The place looks like a scene from a space-adventure movie.

"Over here!" Evan calls. He's putting on a strange-looking space suit.

"Watch this!" Evan says, as he pulls down the goggles and pushes the start button. Suddenly he drops to a crouch. "I'm in a space cruiser on a mission to save the galaxy. My first objective is to destroy the Alpha Romeo space outpost where a group of rogue Federation elite corps has its base."

You jump back as Evan spins, waving his hands wildly in the air. "I got one!" he screams. He ducks and turns to the left. "Four more bearing right down on me!"

BLAM! The suit emits an explosive sound.

"I'm dead!" Evan screams. He falls to the floor.

Trouble on page 12.

24

You point to the virtual-reality suit. "How much is that?"

"Fifty dollars," she answers cheerfully as the two of you walk over to it.

"Hmmm," you say.

You dig into your pocket and fish out a wad of bills and change. Slowly you unfold them: $13.58. It's this week's allowance and lunch money. You figure you can go without school lunch for a month. You'll just eat a big breakfast. "Can I make a down payment and give you the rest before Christmas?"

She frowns. "Well, I'll need to check with the manager," she says. She walks over to a courtesy phone by the door and dials a number.

You hold up the virtual-reality suit and check it over. You desperately want to get the suit for Evan. He's your best friend, and you know it will knock his socks off. The thrill of making his Christmas dream come true outweighs any sense of sacrifice on your part. Besides, you hate school lunch.

The tiny saleswoman returns. "Good news! You can pay in installments or . . ."

Or what? Check it out on page 54.

Evan's legs shake as he sprawls across the van's floor. A muted scream comes from his locked jaw. You see panic in his eyes.

Quickly you wrap him in the ratty old blanket that your dog sleeps on when he's riding in the van. Then you take your sleeve and try to rub off the makeup. It won't come off.

It's as if his skin has been permanently stained!

Slowly Evan gives you a big hug.

You take the dull edge of the knife and pry open Evan's mouth. Inside you see an intricate set of metal braces that are keeping his jaw locked shut.

You find a pair of pliers in the glove compartment and pry enough of the braces off Evan's teeth to allow him to speak.

"Thanks," he gasps.

But are your problems solved?

Uh-oh. Head to page 87.

26

"Uh, I think my friend is stuck in that ride over there." You point toward the door across the room.

"Hmmm." The elf nods knowingly. "I'll see what I can do." He pulls a gold cord hanging behind him, and a bell rings.

Before you can blink, another elf pops up beside you. He salutes. "Yes, sir!"

"Help this customer, pronto!" The manager goes back to his work.

"I'm Gumbo," the elf says cheerfully.

You explain your problem.

Gumbo nods. "Follow me." He pauses. "But first, put this on." He hands you some army fatigues. "It's kind of dirty where we're going. You'll want to protect your clothes."

"Okay," you tell him, accepting the fatigues. You put them on.

Gumbo leads you to a back room full of green, red, and blue vats. They're brimming with a gelatinlike substance.

"Yuck," you say, pointing to the vats. "It'd be really gross to fall in one of those."

"It happens," Gumbo replies. "More often than you can imagine," he adds ominously.

Go to page 40.

But the chute seems longer than last time. You keep sliding down and down. You expect at any moment to burst through the end into the ball pit. But you don't.

You fall for hours and hours. The darkness and the heat are intense. You start to sweat. Then the temperature begins to cool down, and you start getting a chill. As you and Evan continue to fall, you get colder and colder, until you finally slide out onto a giant pile of snow.

"Snow?" you shriek. "It isn't snowing in Freeville."

"Where are we?" Evan screams pathetically.

Find out on page 49.

"Uh, yeah," you say. "I was wondering if you people could help me."

"Sure, my name's Roger Kelly," the voice says cheerfully.

You explain what's happened to the Camperdown Maple.

Mr. Kelly is outraged. He wants to stage a protest in front of the toy store over Thanksgiving weekend as well as circulate a petition.

"I suggest you go to your town clerk's office and get a copy of the building permit to see how they got permission to construct their store around the tree."

You gulp. You've never been to town hall before.

If you're determined to protest, turn to page 6.

If you bag the protest, flip to page 47.

You hang back. You're pretty upset that the town has let the Camperdown Maple be enclosed by a building. It's your favorite tree, and now you can't see or enjoy it. The majestic maple has been turned into a silly toy. Its great, spreading limbs now look more like an amusement park than one of Freeville's natural wonders. And how could a building this large go up in one week?

Out of principle you want to boycott the toy castle, but it does look cool.

*If you decide to go in,
turn to page 50.*

*If you decide to stand by your principles,
turn to page 64.*

30

You approach Evan after school the next day, but he seems strangely distracted. When you mention the Wally Wimp game, he stares at you as if you're crazy. "What Wally Wimp game?" he asks.

You decide not to pursue the matter. Over the next few weeks, you see Evan less and less. He always seems to be preoccupied with something and never has time to hang out after school.

The week before Christmas, he stops coming to school altogether. You're worried. He is your best friend, after all, even if he has been acting weird lately. You decide to go over to his house after school. When you get there, the shades are all drawn.

You ring the doorbell.

After about a minute, you ring it again and wait. And wait. And wait. Nobody answers.

You decide to check the backyard. Maybe Evan is outside playing with his dog, Bubba, and can't hear the doorbell. You walk around the house and climb over the chain-link fence that surrounds the backyard.

Find out if he answers on page 51.

You hobble to the bathroom for a quick shower. Just as you step under the water, your mom bursts into the bathroom.

"Mom!" you yell in exasperation. How many times have you told her not to walk in on you when you're in the bathroom? "I need privacy!" She never listens.

"I'm not looking. I'm not looking," your mom says as she covers her eyes. "You've got a phone call." She holds out the cordless phone.

"Can't it wait?" you ask impatiently.

"It's Evan," she says. "I think you want to take this. Now dry off and take the phone." She leaves it on the sink as she walks out.

You wrap a towel around your waist and grab the phone. "Evan! Are you all right?"

"Yeah, yeah," Evan says casually. "I got lost in the store. When they closed, I was locked in for the night."

"Really?" you say. "Cool! I'd like to be locked up with all those toys."

"It *was* pretty boss," Evan admits. "Did you know they've got lasers and holographic targets?"

Check out page 65.

"What?" You give him a puzzled look, but he just waves you over to the cart.

"Bring these toys to the loading dock," he says. "It's down that hall." He points to a door at the other end of the room.

You nod and grab the cart. You push it down the hall, but you can't find the door to the loading dock. There are no signs on the doors along the hall.

What should you do?

If you go back to the storage room, go to page 20.

If you decide to press on, turn to page 9.

"Level thirteen?" you reply with excitement. You can't stand the idea of Evan being better than you at something. You always beat him. That's what makes him such a terrific friend. He doesn't care if he loses. "Okay, let's go." The two of you head for Evan's.

Evan lets you go first on Wally Wimp while he makes a phone call. He returns about fifteen minutes later.

"Who'd you call?" you ask.

Evan hesitates, as if he doesn't want to say. "Just the toy store. I wanted to know when they close. I thought I'd get my dad to come over and check it out with me after dinner."

"Your dad hates shopping," you remind Evan.

Evan comes up close behind you to look over your shoulder. "Maybe."

"Watch this," you say, as you make Wally outmaneuver a dozen charging mountain goats. But Wally Wimp tumbles off the side of the mountain. He's falling . . . falling . . . *CRACK!* Suddenly *you're* falling!

Better go to page 48.

34

Outside the door stand a dozen little men and women dressed in green outfits with red trim. On their feet are shoes with toes that curl up. Some of the men and women are bleeding. All of them are carrying machine guns.

Santa turns to his elves. "Are Donner and Vixen and Prancer and Dancer and the rest of the reindeer outside?"

"Even Rudolph!" the elf in front answers. "But we're going to have to blast our way out of here."

"We were able to fight our way in, but the evil elves have regrouped," adds a short, rosy-cheeked woman.

"Look!" another elf shouts.

Just then a dozen mechanical clowns smash through the wall, firing squirt guns.

"That's not water!" Santa screams.

You and Santa's helpers retreat through the broken door as Santa hurls stuffed animals at the clowns.

The room fills with smoke as the stuffed animals that were soaked by the squirt guns burst into flames.

Hurry to page 57.

36

Behind the right door you find an escalator going up. It's painted all the colors of the rainbow. You step on. Suddenly whistles scream, bells clang, and all sorts of colored lights begin to flash. You can't see where the moving stairs end. They just rise up and up. You ride and ride and ride. You seem to go on forever. Finally you reach the top.

As you step off, you can't see where you're walking. It's totally dark and quiet. Suddenly the silence is broken by an eerie laugh.

"HA! HA! HA! HA! HA! HA!" It sounds like something you'd hear in a fun house. Before you can get your bearings, the floor disappears from under you. You're falling!

With a thump, you bounce on some sort of cushioned mat and roll toward a spinning wheel that looks like something a hypnotist would use to put you under.

You can't take your eyes off the wheel. The blues, pinks, yellows, greens, and reds seem to be pulling you in. Something in the back of your brain tells you to look away. You struggle to avert your gaze.

Turn to page 15.

"Evan!" you scream. You start toward Evan when out of the corner of your eye you see the gunslinger turn toward you.

Desperate, you grab a laser gun and duck behind the table.

"Draw!" the gunslinger shouts, and fires. The table splinters.

You fire wide to the left and explode a pile of blocks.

"Too slow!" the gunslinger drawls again.

You scramble on your hands and knees behind a stack of dolls.

The gunslinger spots you and shouts, "Draw!"

BOOM! Doll parts fly in all directions. You fire dead-on and hit the gunslinger in his chest.

"Oh, you got me, pardner," he gasps before he disintegrates.

Hurry to page 68.

38

Your mom immediately spots someone she recognizes. She drags you over to him. It's Mayor Smith, and he's riding a toy train around in a circle. He's dressed in a wool suit and tie, but something about his eyes doesn't look right. He's covered with the same glitter that's on your mom. It looks very festive.

Your mom begins to lecture the mayor about violations of town policy and disturbing the peace. But Mayor Smith continues to ride the train without acknowledging your mom. In fact, he acts as if he doesn't even see her. He just sits on the caboose with an idiotic grin plastered on his face.

"Mayor Smith, this is ridiculous," your mom begins. She's about to grab the mayor by his lapels when she notices a shelf filled with all kinds of dolls. As if she's suddenly been hypnotized, she walks away from the mayor, sits on the floor, and begins to play with the dolls.

This is not good. Go to page 59.

You crinkle your brow and give him a sideways glance. You wonder what he's thinking, but you're still too upset to find out. Instead you wave and say, "Yeah, tomorrow." You walk toward home.

When you get home, you head for your room and attack the pile of homework Mrs. Loggia has loaded you down with. Normally homework is the absolute last thing you do during the day, but right now it seems better than thinking about Evan lying to you.

You spend the rest of the evening in your room and only come out for a quick supper. Hours after you've gone to bed, a rock is thrown through your bedroom window. Shards of glass scatter across the floor. A chill breeze whips into your room.

Startled, you get up and look out the window.

Flip to page 61.

40

"We dye life-size action figures in these vats," Gumbo tells you. "We're the only store that sells them."

For some reason Gumbo's response makes you nervous. All you want is to find Evan. "Evan's not back here," you protest. "He's stuck in that ride on the main floor."

"This is a shortcut," Gumbo explains. "If he's stuck, we can reach him more easily from here." He leads you up a flight of stairs and across the catwalk over the vats. You hold on tightly to the railing.

Gumbo waves you over to a tiny door at the end of the catwalk. The two of you crawl through. You find yourself near the middle of the giant chute.

"Evan!" you call.

"Help me!" Evan responds faintly.

You crawl up the chute toward Evan's voice. Gumbo follows you.

"We're coming," you say reassuringly, awkwardly gripping the sides of the chute. It takes about ten minutes, but you finally see Evan hanging from the rafters above a huge hole in the chute's floor.

Find out why on page 70.

When you get to Evan's house, his mom opens the door.

"Is Evan home yet, Mrs. Tomchin?" you ask politely.

She shakes her head. "Doesn't he usually walk home with you?"

You nod and explain that the two of you were separated at the new toy castle surrounding the Camperdown Maple.

"I'm sure he'll be home soon," Mrs. Tomchin says reassuringly. "I'll have him call you when he gets in."

"Thanks, Mrs. Tomchin," you reply, and head home.

That night Evan doesn't call. When you go to bed, you decide you'll chew him out at school tomorrow.

It seems as if you've just fallen asleep when you're startled awake by a sharp banging on your bedroom door. Your mom is calling you.

What's up? Find out on page 18.

Your home, your mom and dad, your ob-
noxious little sister, your school, and your entire life. It's all gone! Wiped away like a clean
slate!

Two fat, wart-covered elves come up to you.
The shorter of the two grabs your hand and
shakes it. "Congratulations! You've passed the
grade. You're now ready to become a toy."

Both elves bend over, laughing and joking
hideously. They think their joke is really
funny. You, on the other hand, don't even hear
it. You're too caught up in tossing your stone
one more time.

The taller elf peels back your eyelids and
shines a light in your face. "Another one's
ready!" he shouts over his shoulder.

You're quickly placed on a cart with about a
dozen other kids. You all sit quietly. The cart is
pulled toward a door at the other end of the
room.

Where are you going? Find out on page 85.

"The one that opened yesterday," you tell him.

The clerk shakes his head. "No new businesses have opened since July." He goes back to reading the lunch menu for the local coffee shop.

You glance at Evan. Something smells fishy. You both quickly back out of the clerk's office.

"We've got to stop these people," you say, as the two of you stand on the sidewalk in front of town hall.

"Why?" Evan replies. "It's a pretty cool store. Why not enjoy it?"

"You're so lazy," you reply. "Don't you have any sense of civic responsibility?"

"The only responsibility I feel is toward my stomach," Evan says, rubbing it gleefully. He leads you down the street to Misha's Candy Store.

"Sodas on me," you say, hoping you can maybe bribe Evan into helping you. Then you realize you're broke. Embarrassed, you try diversionary tactics. "On second thought, let's check out the toy store one last time and see if we can sniff out anything."

See if your ploy works on page 55.

Their little engines rev in unison. Then they attack. Hundreds and hundreds of little windup cars race toward you.

You try to back out of the room and slam the door shut. But they're too fast. Like one massive organism, they crowd you out of the room and into the hallway. You leave the cart standing in front of the door and run.

You dash back toward the storage room, but the cars are fast. They're gaining on you. All you can do is hope they wind down before they reach you.

But that doesn't happen. In seconds the cars catch up to you. They run over you repeatedly, until the thousands of tiny wheels have the same effect as four life-size tires.

You're crushed to a pulp. What a pathetic way to die. Run over by windup toys.

The End

Relieved, you explain to the police what happened. Two officers hop into a cruiser and head over to the house where the owners of the new toy shop live. When the police arrive, the owners have already cleared out.

A few weeks later, an item appears on the back page of the *Freeville News Ledger:*

TOY SHOP TERROR

Dec. 23—The owners of a toy shop in Freeville have been apprehended while attempting to cross the border into Canada. According to authorities, a group of a dozen small-statured toy makers were trying to escape a warrant for their arrest on the grounds of making lethal toys and selling them for Christmas. . . .

The End

You decide not to start any trouble at town hall. The next day at school you run into Evan after English class.

"Wow!" Evan yells across the hallway. "That's all I have to say."

You stare at him, confused.

"Wow!" Evan repeats.

"Wow, what?" you ask, getting a little impatient.

"Wow, the toy shop," Evan answers. "That new toy store is awesome. It has the coolest stuff I've ever seen. There's one thing there that I've gotta have."

"What?" you ask excitedly, forgetting your earlier reservations.

Evan spreads his arms in the crowded hallway and smacks a kid in the face.

"Hey!" the kid yells.

"Sorry," Evan apologizes. "Anyway, it's this huge virtual-reality game that's actually a complete suit. It makes you feel like you're really there!"

What? Go to page 73.

48

Evan has just whacked you in the head with a crystal candlestick!

Bright violet stars, sizzling pink circles, and a weird collection of colors and shapes flash before your eyes like a crazy kaleidoscope. Your ears are ringing, and your head feels as if someone has been pounding on it with a sledgehammer. Without opening your eyes, you try to stand up. But you're too dizzy.

Hands lift and carry you to a truck or van. You can't tell which. Groggily you open your eyes. You're surrounded by elflike people from the toy castle.

CRACK! Something hard hits you on the head again.

You pass out.

Flip to page 19.

In front of you stands a tiny redbrick cottage. A small curl of smoke drifts out of the chimney.

The cottage door opens, and a smiling little old lady hurries out. "Oh my!" she exclaims, helping you up. "You must be cold! Let's get you inside."

She leads you and Evan into the cottage and hands you each a steaming cup of hot chocolate.

"Where are we?" you blurt out as you warm your hands on your cup.

The old lady smiles. For the first time you get a good look at her. She looks kind of familiar. Sweet. But she seems a little nervous. She's dressed in a red velvet dress with white fur trim.

"Why, you're at the North Pole, of course," she says, clapping her hands.

"Yeah, right," you answer sarcastically. "And you're Mrs. Claus."

Turn to page 67.

You run to catch up to Evan. He's already halfway across the drawbridge. You push and shove your way around the crush of people. It's a good thing you're thin and small.

"You sure you want to eat this?" you ask Evan, as he stoops over to take a bite of the drawbridge. Your feet squish into the spongy gingerbread.

"Sure," Evan answers, his mouth full. "Why not?"

"Well, people have been walking on it," you say. "It's disgusting!"

Evan shrugs. "I've eaten worse." You look around and see that everyone else is eating the gingerbread, too.

You and Evan head into the castle. The smell of sugar and ginger is everywhere. "This smells better than any bakery!" you exclaim.

At the door, you are greeted by a man with pointy ears who is wearing a green smock, feathered cap, and red shoes that curl up. "Welcome! Welcome! We have the finest hand-made toys available. Come in and enjoy!"

You and Evan smile and enter.

"He looks like an elf," Evan jokes.

Hurry to page 80.

The yard is empty. That's weird. The Tomchins always let Bubba out into the backyard when they leave the house.

You walk up the steps to the deck and peer through the sliding glass doors that open into the TV room. You see movement in the shadows.

Bang! Bang! You hit your fist against the glass, hoping to get the person's attention. "Evan!" you call.

No one answers.

You try the door, and it slides open. You step into the room. It's eerily quiet. Almost too quiet. You can't even hear the hum of the fridge in the kitchen. Cautiously you tiptoe through the house.

"Evan?" you whisper. The house is still too quiet. You walk down the hall to check upstairs, but you don't get as far as the stairs.

A dozen elves leap over the banister and pin you to the ground! "If you've quiet, we won't kill you," a fat elf barks. "We're just waiting until after Christmas. Then it'll be safe enough to escape without Santa tracking us down."

You nod.

Flip to page 13.

You decide not to say anything. It was probably just a crazy dream, anyway. Several weeks later, on Christmas morning, a beautifully wrapped box appears under the tree. And inside is your very own copy of Wally Wimp!

You turn to your mom and dad. "Thanks!"

"For what?" your parents respond.

"This game," you reply. "You said they were sold out at the store."

Your dad shakes his head. "We didn't buy any game." You dig through the wrapping paper. The tag reads:

THANKS FOR ALL YOUR HELP!

MERRY CHRISTMAS, SANTA.

Your eyes bug out. Was it true? Did rogue elves really kidnap you and Santa? As you're thinking about this, your dad gives your mom a wink. She winks back. But you don't see any of this.

You can't wait to run over to Evan's house and tell him. But wait. If you really *were* kidnapped, was Evan really hypnotized by the evil elves?

The End

She tears the flap off one of the boxes and writes a note on it. "Here," she says as she hands you the flap. "Take this to the front desk. They'll give you the toy you want."

"Thank you," you say enthusiastically and hurry back to the sales floor. As you do, you read the note:

This person has worked off the owed amount.

You're not sure why she did this, but you're really glad. Not only do you not want to work, there is something creepy about this place. And you don't want to hang around and find out what. Especially after that little guy's earlier warning.

The End

54

Or you can spend four afternoons stocking toys in the storeroom to pay off the balance.

This sounds really cool. You glance over at Evan. He's involved in a passionate conversation with another sales elf. You have to make up your mind fast. It would be neat to actually work in a toy store. But at the same time, can you pull it off without Evan catching on? The two of you hang out together after school every day.

You vow to keep it a secret. "You got a deal!" A wide smile spreads across your face. Evan will never be able to top this, you think.

Sounds good. Go to page 75.

"Great idea!" Evan says enthusiastically. "I really want to check the place out one more time before you get it shut down and ruin everything.

"But I'm really thirsty," he adds. "Let's get sodas first."

"I'm broke," you say sheepishly. You pull out your pockets for emphasis.

Evan waves you away. "No sweat. I'm buying." He slaps a twenty-dollar bill on the counter.

Your eyes bug out. You've never seen Evan with this kind of money. "Where'd you get that?" you gasp.

"Early Christmas present from my uncle Melvin." Evan grabs a licorice stick as well.

You look at Evan suspiciously. He doesn't have an uncle called Melvin. Why is he lying? Should you confront him on it? Or should you let it go and order a soda? Is it really that big a deal?

Confront Evan on page 8.

Overlook his lie on page 62.

56

You're left-handed, so naturally you reach for the left doorknob.

As you step inside the room, you see a huge, ten-foot-high cake. A small woman with pointed ears, wearing a green dress with red trim, is standing atop a stepladder cutting slices.

Dozens of kids are stuffing their faces with cake and playing hopscotch and jacks and dodgeball. The room is a humongous playground. But it doesn't make sense. The castle isn't big enough to hold a room this size.

Just then, the elf woman hands you a slice of cake. As you stare at the waves of icing, all your resistance melts. You immediately shove your face into the slice.

Chow down on page 11.

You duck out through the door with Santa right behind you. The elves in front blast their guns furiously as evil elves appear.

You stumble and fall. Luckily Santa lifts you by the seat of your pants and drags you through a window.

Outside, Santa's sleigh is waiting. Everyone leaps in, and the reindeer take off.

"That was close," you gasp. You wipe your brow with your hand and see blood smeared across it. Behind you the toy castle and the Camperdown Maple are engulfed in flames.

The next day you wake up and check your forehead in the mirror. There's no cut. You run to the toy store. It's not there! In fact, the Camperdown Maple looks the way it used to. There's no sign of any building ever having been built around it. And none of its branches are burned.

Obviously, this doesn't make sense. But do you really want to try to explain it to someone? They're going to think you're nuts. On the other hand, you could tell Evan. *He* might not think you're crazy.

Tell Evan on page 30.

Keep quiet on page 52.

"You've been a bad dolly," your mom scolds the first doll in a childlike voice. "You wet your panties. Now I'm going to have to change you." She lays the doll on the floor and begins to unbutton its clothes.

What is going on?

All you see are adults completely obsessed with toys. And every one of them is covered with that glitter. Your teacher, Mrs. Loggia, is playing jacks with Principal Margolis. The two police officers who came to your house are playing pat-a-cake in the middle of the ball pit, while Mrs. Tomchin is screaming that she's king of the hill from a branch of the Camperdown Maple.

You shake your head in disbelief. Has every adult in town gone nuts? That's when a giant jack-in-the-box pops open and startles you.

"Not again!" you exclaim as the jack pops out. But what startles you even more is the jack's face. It looks exactly like Evan, but with clown makeup! You approach the jack-in-the-box with caution. You don't trust anything in this crazy place.

To your surprise, it calls out your name!

Quick! Go to page 66.

A van is idling on the street in front of your house. The person in the passenger seat looks vaguely like Evan, but you know it can't be. You grab the towel you left on the floor after your shower this morning and shove it into the hole in the broken window.

"What kind of loser throws rocks at people's windows?" you mutter. Still half asleep, you climb back in bed and pull the covers over your head.

At the same time, a ladder is gently propped up against your window. A small, furry teddy bear pushes the towel onto the floor. He climbs through your window and waves for the others behind him to follow. About thirty bears gather quietly at the end of your bed. Without making a sound, they crawl onto your blanket.

You stir as your blanket slips halfway off.

The cute teddy bears freeze. You snuggle deeper into your bed.

Turn to page 74.

Even though you're surprised that Evan would actually lie, you don't want to confront him. Instead, you try to enjoy your soda, since this is the first time Evan has ever opened his wallet and treated. Unfortunately, the fact that Evan is lying to you ruins the experience. You're disappointed in him and decide to go home. You don't want to hang out with him if he can't tell the truth.

"I've got homework to do," you say, as an excuse.

"You can't put it off until after supper?" Evan asks. "What about the protest?"

"We can do it tomorrow," you answer. "I think we can get Mrs. Loggia to help us organize it after school. She's always talking about the environment in class."

A worried look crosses Evan's face. He scowls. He's just upset that you're ditching him.

"See ya tomorrow," he mumbles in a distracted way.

Turn to page 39.

"What can we do?" you ask.

"Wait it out," Santa says. "At some point my good elves will figure out where I am and come to my rescue. I just hope it happens before Christmas. I hate to think of all the kids who depend on me not getting any presents."

You smirk. "You can't be Santa Claus."

"But I am." He tells you your name and recites the items on your Christmas lists over the past few years. Then he mentions the broken window a few weeks back.

"Yeah, right," you answer, still a bit skeptical. You fall into a pile of cuddly rabbits and decide to let the old man have his fantasy.

Suddenly a cacophony of noise rises just outside the room.

Someone bangs on the door. You hear a faint voice. "Santa? Santa? Are you in there?"

At the same time you hear shouting and noises that sound like bullets being fired.

Santa perks up. "Yes! Is that you, Elsnor?"

"Stand back, Santa!" the voice shouts.

BOOM! The door splinters open, clearing the way for the most amazing sight you've seen in your life!

Find out what's beyond the door on page 34.

You tell Evan you'll catch up with him later and head home. In a few minutes, you're walking up to your front door. Inside, you shrug out of your jacket. It drops to the floor in the middle of the hall. You head for the fridge. You want something to eat before you figure out what to do about the Camperdown Maple.

Now you can think. And it takes no time for you to figure out what to do first. You call the state environmental protection agency.

You quickly realize they can't help. The woman who answers the phone has a scratchy, gravelly voice. She sounds as if she has spent too many years breathing environmental waste. The first question she asks is if the Camperdown Maple is a toxic-waste dump.

You flip through the phone book and find the number for Green America. You remember the name from some school presentation. You dial.

"Save the planet, plant a tree," says the man who answers the phone. "May I help you help a tree?"

Go to page 28.

"Do you think you could get us locked in tonight?" you ask excitedly.

"No problema," Evan boasts. "Meet me after school."

Later that afternoon, you and Evan head for the toy shop. Once there, Evan leads you to a utility closet off the main floor. "In here," he says. "They won't find us."

"Great!" you answer. The two of you squeeze into the closet. The overpowering smell of ammonia almost makes you hurl. You pinch your nose, breathe through your mouth, and wait. You're there for hours, listening for the noise in the store to die down.

"You have a watch?" you whisper.

"Nope," Evan says. You both continue to wait.

Your legs begin to fall asleep from standing in one place for so long. You realize that you should have waited and hid just before the store closed. Brilliant planning.

Take action on page 17.

"Evan?" you ask cautiously.

"Yes, yes," it mumbles. "Help me!" His voice sounds as if it's been squeezed through a pinhole.

You can't believe your eyes or ears! There's no doubt that this jack-in-the-box is Evan. "What have they done to you?" you blurt out.

"Help me, help me," the jack-in-the-box pleads. Tears flow from its eyes. It looks as if it's in serious pain.

Without thinking, you drag the jack-in-the-box out the front door. Two elves try to stop you.

"Get away!" you order, swatting at them like flies. You discover that the elves aren't very strong. With a lot of effort, you lift the jack-in-the-box into the back of your mom's van and climb in with it. You've got to figure out a way to set Evan free! You grab the pocketknife your mom keeps in the glove compartment and cut away.

As you tear the fabric away from Evan's body, you discover that he's been tied to a huge spring attached to the bottom of the box. You cut through the ropes, and Evan steps out.

Find out more on page 25.

"Oh, yes," she replies jovially. "I thought you'd never guess!"

Just then you hear a big, booming voice singing "Rudolph, the Red-Nosed Reindeer." The front door bursts open, and a large, round man also dressed in red velvet with white fur trim is standing on the doorstep. He gives a hearty laugh, but his eyes are impatient. "Why aren't they in the factory?" he shouts.

"I—I was just sending them over, Kris," Mrs. Claus stammers.

"Well, hop to it," he growls. "We've got a schedule to keep, and the elves have been dropping like flies."

"This way," Mrs. Claus commands. She takes your unfinished cups of hot chocolate away and hurriedly stacks them in the sink. Then she motions you to follow her.

"We're going back outside?" you ask.

Mrs. Claus bites her lip. "You won't be outside for long."

You and Evan follow her to a large hall where dozens of kids are hard at work making toys. She leads you to a worktable and teaches you how to assemble wooden trains.

Turn to page 82.

You lean against a large gingerbread house and catch your breath. "Too close," you gasp.

You hear the black box begin to hum again. You dive for it and knock the switch off. The last thing you want is another gunslinger to fight.

Slowly you work your way across the shop to Evan. You can hear him gurgling.

"Help," he says weakly. Miraculously, he is still alive. You drag him out of the shop and flag down a passing car.

The driver calls 911 on his cell phone. The ambulance and the police arrive together. The sirens wake up the entire town.

"Is he going to make it?" you ask the EMS worker.

"Sure," she answers as she lifts Evan into the ambulance. "He's just in shock."

Go to page 46.

Without thinking, you grab the jack's hand and pull it out of the purse. Gripped tight in its fist is the woman's wallet. You shake the wallet free. It falls to the floor.

Just then the woman turns and sees her wallet at your feet.

"Hellllp!" she screams above the din of toys and tunes. "I'm being robbed!"

"But—but—" you stammer. "I wasn't . . ." Quickly you realize that you won't be able to explain. How can you convince anyone that the jack-in-the-box is a pickpocket?

You turn and dash through the crowd. You think you're heading for the drawbridge, but you get turned around and end up in front of two identical mirrored doors. The door on the right has the word "right" painted on it. The door on the left shows the word "left."

You glance over your shoulder and see the woman pointing at you. You have to act fast. But which door should you go through? Left? Right?

If you choose left, go to page 56.

If you choose right, go to page 36.

"The chute is broken," you gasp. You move toward Evan and grab his arm. But just as you do, Gumbo gives you a hard push!

You scramble to catch your balance, but instead you fall through the hole in the chute, dragging Evan with you. That's when you notice that it *isn't* a hole at all. It's a trapdoor. And the trapdoor is right over a vat of green gunk!

You and Evan struggle to stay afloat, but the green gelatin pulls you farther and farther down until you can no longer breathe.

The green gunk covers your entire body.

You're smothered!

After about an hour Gumbo pulls you and Evan from the vat. He poses you in action positions and expertly wraps your hands around toy guns. Within seconds, your bodies take on the hardness of plastic. You and Evan are now part of a life-size collection of figurines that a retired general has ordered for his grandson's Christmas present.

The general has insisted the toys be lifelike. And they couldn't be any more lifelike than you and Evan.

Except if you were still alive!

The End

Santa Claus! No, you tell yourself, you're hallucinating. First you thought you were in the video game. Now you think you're at the North Pole. But the old man has ruddy cheeks, a long white beard, and a twinkle in his eye!

"There, there," he says. "Don't worry. We'll get you out of this."

"Get—get out of what?" you stammer.

The jolly-looking man glances around the room. "Out of here. Out of this storage room in the evil elves' castle."

"Elves' castle!" you exclaim. "You must be nuts!"

"You're mistaken," the old man answers. "I'm not nuts. I'm Santa Claus!"

You grab your hair and try to pull it out. "Where's Evan?" you yell.

"Calm down," Santa says soothingly.

You scramble on your hands and knees to the other side of the room. "Get away from me!" you scream. You're not real. You're . . ."

Santa comes over to you and pinches your cheek hard.

"Ouch!" you yell. That pinch hurt. He *is* real. "What is this place?"

You'll see on page 81.

"Cool!" You bounce on the balls of your feet. You can't wait to try it out.

"And the best part is it's only fifty bucks!" Evan says.

You whistle. No video game is that cheap. Especially not the one you've been begging your parents for: Wally Wimp. No store in town has it. It's been sold out for months.

You and Evan agree to meet after school and head over to the toy shop.

Toy monkeys and clowns move back and forth across tightropes strung underneath the ceiling. Kids play with pogo sticks, trains, dolls, and dozens of games and toys you don't recognize. A giant teddy bear is handing out candy canes while cute elflike people dressed in green outfits with red trim scurry about assisting kids and answering questions.

Cool stuff on page 23.

Once you fall deeper into sleep, the teddy bears surround your body and pummel you with their soft fists. While your skin doesn't bruise, your internal organs are pounded to a pulp. Two of the bears grab a pillow and press it against your face. You die quietly in your sleep.

The bears slip through the window and return to the van idling out front. Evan is standing by the van's open back door, waving the bears in. When the last bear climbs up, he pulls the door closed and hops back into the passenger seat.

The van heads across town to the town clerk's home. The same thing happens to him.

In the following weeks, the police can find no leads in their investigation of these and similar crimes. There are no fingerprints at any of the crime scenes, and there is no evidence . . . except for little tufts of teddy bear fur found around the bodies.

The End

The next day you arrive at the toy shop castle after school. You had a surprisingly easy time shaking Evan. He didn't want to hang out. You thank your lucky stars.

"Excuse me," you say to the first little guy dressed in green that you see. "I'm here for the stockroom position."

He smiles. "Yes, of course! Follow me."

He leads you through a door that's disguised as a bookcase into a storage room. Inside are stacks of awesome toys and games. A dozen short people dressed in green are at work stacking toys and putting them in boxes.

You wonder where these people come from. They're all short and look alike. You turn to your guide. "Where are you from? Are you all related?"

He laughs and motions you over to a large cart loaded with boxes. "If you stay here long enough, you just might find out." Then he cups his hand over his mouth. "But I'd advise you not to," he whispers.

Huh? Hurry to page 32.

"Maybe you should let us return it," you tell Mrs. Tomchin. You're a bit worried about her going to the toy castle alone.

"Yeah, Mom. I'll bring it back," Evan says.

"Okay. But do it first thing tomorrow," Mrs. Tomchin tells him.

The next day, you and Evan bring the suit to the toy castle.

"What was the problem?" a customer-service elf asks.

"It took control of me when I put it on!" Evan tells him.

The elf nods. "We've had several complaints about this suit already." He takes the suit and carefully folds it up. "I can give you a refund. Or maybe you'll find something else?"

Evan shakes his head. "I'll take a refund."

You wait as the elf fills out some paperwork. He then hands Evan several crisp bills.

"Thanks for your help," Evan tells the elf as the two of you exit the store.

"You're welcome," says the elf. As soon as you leave, he motions to one of the sales elves. "Put this out on the sales floor!" he instructs. "And mark it down fifty percent!"

The End

Two police officers are standing in the living room. The crackle of their walkie-talkies hurts your ears. You're still not completely awake. You shake your head, hoping this is all a dream. But it isn't.

"Please sit," one of the officers says. He's really skinny, so skinny that you wonder how he could pass the physical.

You sit.

"I'm Officer McAvoy," he says, "and this is Officer Stein." He points to the female officer standing beside him. She looks more like a cop than McAvoy does. She has a serious, no-nonsense expression on her face. "We'd like to know exactly when you last saw your friend."

You nod. "At that new toy store on Maple Street," you answer. You explain how you were separated when Evan tried the ride.

The two officers glance knowingly at each other. "We suspected as much," Officer Stein says. "In fact—"

"What do you mean?" your mom interrupts.

Officer McAvoy holds up his hand as if to say, *Don't ask.* "We'll be in touch," he says, and he and Officer Stein back out the front door.

Now what? Turn to page 84.

78

You spot one of the castle's elves sitting at a raised desk. He looks as if he's the store manager. He's really busy, but you interrupt him anyway.

"Excuse me!" you shout.

The elf peers down over his high desk at you. He has the ugliest nose you've ever seen. It's huge. A giant wart sprouts from the end, with two black hairs growing out of its tip. "Yeah?" he replies gruffly.

You shrink back. This guy doesn't look very friendly. You're not so sure you want his help.

If you decide to try someone else, go to page 7.

If you persist, flip back to 26.

On your way over to Evan's, you notice a doll walking stiff-legged along the sidewalk with what looks like a child's dress in its mouth. Its blue eyes are spinning in opposite directions, and an eerie growl rumbles from its throat. The doll is totally weird.

But not as weird as what you see in the middle of the next block.

At the bottom of someone's driveway, a kid is stretched out on his back while a large remote-control car runs back and forth over him.

You shake your head in disbelief. To be killed by the remote-control car you get for Christmas—that's brutal. Truly brutal.

In the next block you turn up Evan's driveway and skid a cool fishtail. You dash up to the front door and ring the bell. A few seconds pass, and the front door explodes. *KABOOM!*

You're thrown off the front stoop by the explosion. A bloodcurdling scream brings you back to your senses. Evan, dressed in some kind of space suit, comes leaping through the smoking doorway.

He aims some sort of laser gun at you.

What do you do? Hurry to page 22.

"Yeah." Your stomach rumbles. "Santa's elves must be setting up franchises."

Your eyes drink up the incredibly delicious-looking castle. You want some candy and gingerbread now, but you're nervous about eating unwrapped candy. Your mom's voice in the back of your head keeps repeating itself: "Don't take unwrapped candy from anyone! You never know what's in it."

You try to distract yourself by looking at all the amazing toys spinning and hopping and skipping and flying around the room. Music fills the air.

Bang! Bang! Bang!

Startled, you turn and see a six-foot-high clown banging a little drum. It's the biggest windup clown you've ever seen! And it stops right in front of you. You're surprised at how real it looks. You turn the key in its back and wind the clown up again. It goes off across the floor, banging its drum.

You shake your head in disbelief. "That clown felt like a real person!" you exclaim to Evan. But Evan's not behind you. He's gone off to look at a mountain of teddy bears.

Investigate more on page 14.

"We're being held hostage by a group of rogue elves that I cast out of the North Pole when they tried to take over," Santa tells you.

"You've got to be kidding," you protest. "I was just playing a video game at my friend's house."

A serious scowl crosses Santa's face. "Does your friend have shaggy brown hair?"

You nod.

"Is he about this tall?" Santa asks, holding his hand up to the same height as Evan. "And does he wear a torn jean jacket with a patch that says 'Munch On' stitched to the right shoulder?"

"That's Evan!" you shout.

Santa shakes his head sadly. "He was with the elves when they brought you here. They've brainwashed him."

"This can't be happening," you cry as you jump up and run to the door. "Get me out of here!"

Santa sinks into a pile of teddy bears. "It's no use. They're not going to let you out. I've been in here for at least a week."

Find out more on page 63.

"What's going on?" you ask the kid at the table next to you.

"Don't you get it?" she says unhappily. "Santa isn't the jolly fellow you meet at the mall. He's a tyrant. And we're his slaves."

"Slaves?" you repeat.

"We're taking the place of elves," she explains. "Most of them were worked until they dropped dead. Now we're their replacements."

The End

You and your mom stare at each other. "Now, what exactly is this toy store?" your mom asks with a serious look on her face.

"It's this really cool new castle that's built around the Camperdown Maple," you reply. "They make all their own toys, and the people who work there look like elves."

"Elves?" your mom repeats. "You've got to be kidding."

"No," you protest. "They even have pointy ears."

Your mom goes to the closet and pulls out your coats. "Let's go investigate this place."

Cool, you think. It's two A.M., and you're going on an adventure. What's gotten into your mom? She never does neat things like this.

But then you get an eerie feeling. If Evan disappeared at the elves' toy castle, then this store is dangerous. You don't want to be snooping around it at two A.M. You would prefer to wait until the light of day.

If you decide to go along, turn to page 21.

If you convince your mom to wait, turn to page 16.

Everyone's unloaded in a massive hall that looks like a huge workshop. You are led over to a workbench where an ancient elf is tinkering with some sort of gizmo that has a long handle. He stands up and begins to attach the gizmo to your head. Then he dresses you in a red uniform with a tall fur hat.

When he's finished, he fishes a walnut out of his pocket and pulls up the handle that now runs down the length of your back. Your jaw automatically opens. He slips the walnut into your mouth and yanks the handle down. Your teeth easily break the shell. The elf separates the shell from the nut meat and eats the walnut.

He slaps you on the back and shouts, "Done!"

Another elf wheels you out to the toy store and places you beside a long row of nutcrackers, all dressed in garish uniforms and tall furry hats. Eventually you are bought by an old woman with a yen for walnuts, and you spend the next ten years cracking nuts.

The End

Without hesitation, you open the left door again and ride the escalator up into the darkness. At the top, you bump into someone standing in the shadows.

"Hey!" the person shouts.

"Evan!" you say, grabbing his shirt. "It's me! What are you doing?"

"I hate dark places," he explains. "And this ride is way too scary. I want to go back down!" He tries to push you aside to climb back down the escalator the wrong way.

"You can't go back," you reply.

"Why can't they turn on some lights?" he complains.

"Follow me," you say as you step forward. "We'll go down the chute together."

Suddenly the quiet is broken.

"HA! HA! HA! HA! HA! HA!"

"Close your eyes!" you yell as the crazy multicolored spinning wheel comes into view.

You glide down the twisting chute. Evan is screaming behind you. The panic in his voice is real, but you're laughing anyway. You love crazy rides like this. You know you'll want to do it again when you reach the end.

Or will you? Turn to page 27.

In the morning the National Guard rescues you and Evan from the parking lot. They shut down the castle. Unfortunately, the adults can't be saved. They've all been turned into automatons that continue to perform the same actions over and over.

The doctors can't stop your mom from playing with dolls. Your teacher and the principal keep playing jacks, while the mayor won't get off the caboose. Mrs. Tomchin lives to play king of the hill. They are all sent to an asylum, where they live out their days sadly repeating the same actions for years. You end up going to live with your grandparents.

Evan joins you. He's lucky to have you for a friend. You're probably the only person who understands why his face is so . . . colorful. The doctors can't find a way to get the clown makeup off.

The End

Both you and Evan nod in complete agreement.

The next day, Mrs. Tomchin returns the virtual-reality suit to the elves' toy castle and discovers that the store has been closed down. Apparently, all the toys sold at the store were made to hurt people. Nearly a third of Freeville was massacred around the Christmas tree the day before. All over town people are trying to pick up the pieces and understand what happened.

You thank your lucky stars that you told your parents you were too old for toys. If only that were true, you think, as you watch a six-year-old playing jacks by herself on the sidewalk in front of your house.

You sit down beside her and challenge her to a game of threesies.

The End